WHEN WILL IT SNOW?

WHEN WILL IT SNOW?

written and illustrated

by

Bruce Hiscock

ATHENEUM BOOKS FOR YOUNG READERS

BOOKS BY BRUCE HISCOCK

Tundra

The Big Rock

The Big Tree

The Big Storm

When Will It Snow?

Atheneum Books for Young Readers
An imprint of Simon & Schuster Books for Young Readers
1230 Avenue of the Americas, New York, NY 10020

The text of this book is set in Meridien Roman.
The illustrations are rendered in watercolor.

First edition

Printed in the United States of America

10 9 8 7 6 5 4 3 2 1

Library of Congress Cataloging-in-Publication Data
Hiscock, Bruce.
When will it snow? / written and illustrated by Bruce Hiscock.—1st ed.
p.   cm.
Summary: A small boy impatiently awaits the first snowfall while the small animals
of the woods prepare for winter.
ISBN 0-689-31937-1
[1. Winter—Fiction.   2. Forest animals—Fiction.   3. Snow—[Fiction.]
I. Title.   PZ7.H615Wh 1995   [E]—dc20   94-9385

To my good friends, and to everyone whose spirits soar when the first snowflakes fall. Special thanks to my nephew Will as Robin.

$\mathcal{T}$he North Country was waiting for winter to begin. The cold
wind had returned, and for days now thick clouds filled the sky.
The clouds moved slowly over the great forests, but so far, not a
single snowflake had fallen. Even high on the hills, the ground
was still bare.

Winter was late, and as another gray morning began, people
wondered, when will it snow?

At the town garage they were ready. The salt barn was filled with road salt, and a mountain of sand stood outside. Freshly painted plows rested beside the huge trucks, just waiting to be hitched on. Inside, the highway crew sipped coffee and talked about last year's blizzards "with drifts as high as your head." They were expecting snow anytime.

Up on the hill, where Robin lived with his mom, they had been expecting snow for weeks now. Well, at least Robin had. Every morning he hopped out of bed, rushed to the window, and peered out at the old meadow, hoping to see it all covered in white.

But today, in the pale light before sunrise, the meadow looked as dull and brown as ever. Robin shook his head. He was tired of waiting. He had a new sled and everything. He was ready for snow!

Across the old meadow a deer mouse was getting ready, too. She had built a thick nest, even before the cold weather came. Now she was busy filling another storage place with seeds. The deer mouse had never seen winter or snow, for she was only three months old. But she knew what to do. She was fully grown and guided by the strong instincts that help all animals survive.

As the day brightened, she hid a few beechnuts away, and then cleaned her whiskers and curled up to sleep.

Robin was just starting his breakfast when a flock of small birds swooped into the birch tree by the kitchen.

"Chick-a-dee-dee-dee," they sang, and pecked hungrily at the seeds. Some of the birds in the flock had lived through the winter before and knew about cold. "Eat, eat, eat," they seemed to say, and cocked their heads as if checking the sky for snow. But all they saw were clouds, and a patch or two of blue.

"When will it snow?" Robin asked his mom as he got ready for school.

"Soon, maybe," she answered. "The weather report said it might snow this afternoon."

"I think it will!" Robin said, and all through the morning he watched the sky.

By midday, though, the clouds were thinning. Only the wind that rustled the grass felt like winter. Beneath the frozen earth of the old meadow, a groundhog slept the season away. He was in deep hibernation and would not wake up until spring. Groundhogs couldn't care less about snow.

When Robin's mother picked him up after school, he was feeling discouraged, let down, and crabby, too. "Mom," he said, "do you think it will ever snow?"

"Oh, Robin," his mom said, smiling. "Of course it will. Let's go buy some extra food, just in case we're snowed in."

"Okay," said Robin, and they bought cocoa and things for soup and pizza. It was dark by the time they got home, for the days were very short now.

That evening began cold and clear. In the forest a snowshoe hare nibbled twigs in the moonlight. The hare's fur had been brown all summer. Now he had grown a new coat that was almost pure white. His big, furry feet were like snowshoes. The hare moved cautiously, stopping to listen for a fox or coyote, and then went back to eating. He was fat and ready for winter.

Farther up the hill a gray fox began her nightly rounds. Thick, speckled fur kept her small body warm, but she was lean and hungry. Last spring she had lost a leg in a trap. She had survived, living on berries and frogs and anything else she could find. Hunting mice and rabbits would be hard this winter, especially in deep snow. The fox sniffed the air, hoping to find the scent of food. Then she set off as high clouds drifted across the sky.

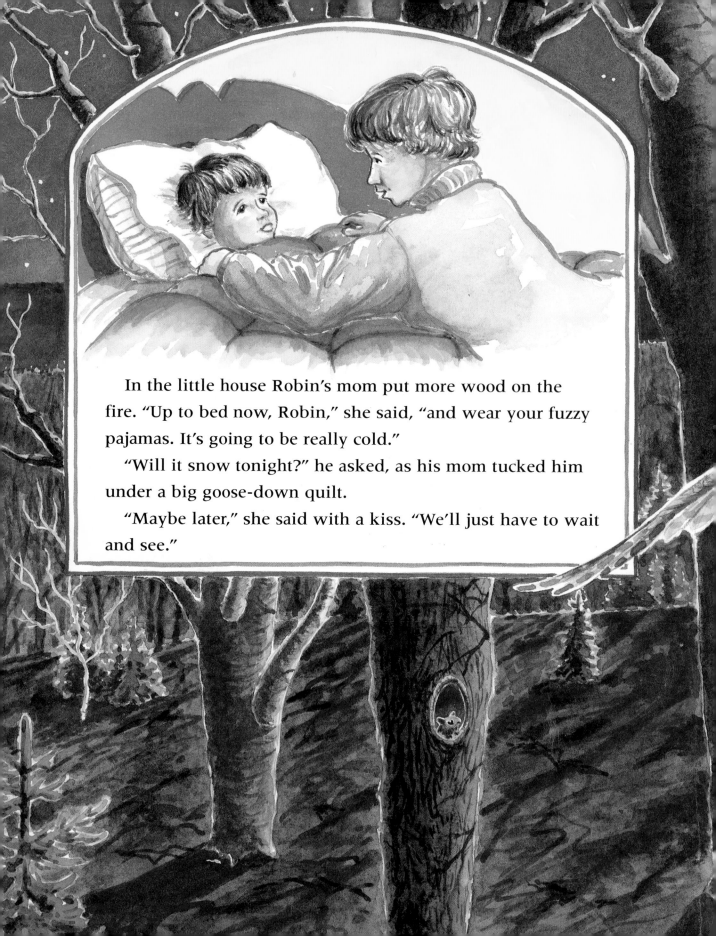

In the little house Robin's mom put more wood on the
fire. "Up to bed now, Robin," she said, "and wear your fuzzy
pajamas. It's going to be really cold."

"Will it snow tonight?" he asked, as his mom tucked him
under a big goose-down quilt.

"Maybe later," she said with a kiss. "We'll just have to wait
and see."

The night was very long. From somewhere in the woods
a barred owl called. "Whoo-whoo . . . wh-whooo." The deer
mouse stopped dead still, its heart racing, as the owl glided
silently overhead.

Not far away the fox slowly tracked the snowshoe hare
through the spruce trees. But when the fox stepped on a dry
leaf, the hare bounded off like a white flash. Robin heard
nothing of this. He was fast asleep, snuggled deep in feathers
like the chickadees.

In the morning the meadow was all white. "Snow!" shouted Robin, and he ran down the stairs and flew out the door. The field sparkled with delicate crystals. It was beautiful, but the crystals were just heavy frost. There was no real snow. Robin came in and put on his clothes very slowly.

"Mom, when will it snow?" he asked again.

"I don't know," she said gently. "Try to be patient, Robin."

"I've been patient!" he said, kicking the rug. "Now I want it to snow."

The day was fair and a bit warmer. After school, Robin helped his mom stack firewood. He liked working outside and tried not to think about his sled or the dumb weather.

When dark clouds appeared in the west, at first Robin ignored them. He wasn't going to be fooled again. But after a while he looked up at the sky and asked, "Are those snow clouds?"

"Well, they might be," his mom replied, laughing.

"They look like snow clouds to me," Robin said, but he wasn't too sure.

As the clouds thickened, the wind dropped away. In the forest the fox awoke early. She sensed something different in the air and began hunting while it was still light.

Robin and his mom had finished their supper. While they were trying to decide what kind of cookies to make, Robin glanced out the window. In the inky darkness tiny white flakes were sifting down from the sky.

It was snowing! Robin raced outside, with his mom close behind. They danced around, catching perfect six-pointed stars on their tongues until their cheeks were red with cold.

Later, they went for a hike across the meadow and into the forest. Snow was coming down fast now, making a faint hissing sound. When they stopped to listen, Robin spotted the three-legged fox in the path up ahead. For once Robin was silent.

"Could we put out some food for that fox?" he asked quietly when they turned toward home.

"Sure," said his mom, "but not too much. I think it can still hunt mice."

As they tramped along, the snowshoe hare heard them coming. The hare lay perfectly still, and they passed right by. In the swirling white world he was almost invisible.

Near the edge of the woods, the deer mouse blinked at the flakes and began making tunnels under the deepening snow.

Robin leaned into the wind as they crossed the meadow again. "We'd better put out food for the mice, too," he called. "You know, tomorrow, when we go sledding." His mom smiled and took his hand.

As they reached their house a familiar noise rumbled up the hill. It was one of the big plows out clearing the road. Winter had come to the North Country at last.